POWER CODERS

THE MISSING PROGRAMMER

L. A. BOWEN

ILLUSTRATED BY JOEL GENNARI

PowerKiDS
press™
New York

Published in 2019 by The Rosen Publishing Group, Inc.
29 East 21st Street, New York, NY 10010

First Edition

Illustrator: Joel Gennari
Interior Layout: Tanya Dellaccio
Editorial Director: Greg Roza
Coding Consultant: Jack daSilva

Cataloging-in-Publishing Data

Names: Bowen, L.A.
Title: The missing programmer / L.A. Bowen.
Description: New York : PowerKids Press, 2019. | Series: Power coders | Includes glossary and index.
Identifiers: ISBN 9781538340226 (pbk.) | ISBN 9781538340219 (library bound) | ISBN 9781538340233 (6 pack)
Subjects: LCSH: Computer programmers–Juvenile fiction. | Coding theory – Juvenile fiction. | Concerts–Juvenile fiction.
Classification: LCC PZ7.B694 Mi 2019 | DDC [E]–dc23

Manufactured in the United States of America

CPSIA Compliance Information: Batch CWPK19. For Further Information contact Rosen Publishing, New York, New York at 1-800-237-9932

CONTENTS

THIS BETTER BE GOOD! IT'S FRIDAY AND IT'S BEAUTIFUL OUTSIDE!

YOU KNOW THERE'S A FREE CONCERT IN THE PARK TONIGHT?

WOOF!

ARE YOU KIDDING ME? THIS CLASS IS GOING TO BE BETTER THAN ANY CONCERT. SAM NORTH IS A CODING LEGEND!

HE'S MY BROTHER'S NUMBER-1 IDOL!

NO ONE KNOWS SAM NORTH'S TRUE IDENTITY. HOW DO YOU KNOW SAM IS A "HE"?

HMM... GOOD POINT.

About the Author:

Sam North—the popular but secretive programmer—is the author of 4 books on coding, including this one, *Bug Fixing*. Despite anonymity, North has developed a large fan base, especially among teens.

I BROUGHT A COPY OF HIS BOOK, *BUG FIXING*.

MS. JONES SAID THAT SAM NORTH WOULD AUTOGRAPH IT FOR ME!

COOL!

I DON'T HAVE A COPY.

MAYBE HE CAN SIGN MY YEARBOOK.

GOOD AFTERNOON, CODERS!

ARE YOU READY TO MEET OUR SPECIAL GUEST?

YES!

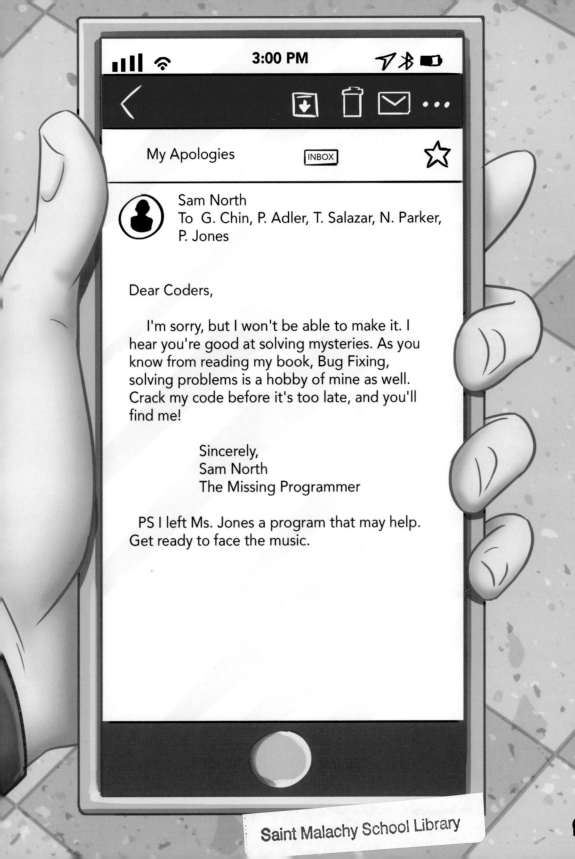

My Apologies INBOX

Sam North
To G. Chin, P. Adler, T. Salazar, N. Parker, P. Jones

Dear Coders,

I'm sorry, but I won't be able to make it. I hear you're good at solving mysteries. As you know from reading my book, Bug Fixing, solving problems is a hobby of mine as well. Crack my code before it's too late, and you'll find me!

Sincerely,
Sam North
The Missing Programmer

PS I left Ms. Jones a program that may help. Get ready to face the music.

Saint Malachy School Library

9

```python
import datetime

#database of performance schedule

database = [

["##-##","Wilson Auditorium"],

["##-##","Junior Music Room"],

["##-##","Grant Park Bandstand"],

["##-##","Melodia Theater"]
]

#counter for whether the item was found

counter=0

while counter ==
0:

#ask user to input date

concertdate = input("Enter a date in mm-dd format:")

for index, sublist
in enumerate(database):


if sublist[0] == concertdate:

if (counter ==0):

print("Junior Music Room")

else:

secretkey = input("Enter code:")

if (secretkey=="######"):

print(database[index][1])
```

Enter a date in mm-dd format:

WHAT DATE SHOULD WE USE?

WHY NOT TODAY'S DATE?

AFTER ALL, HE WAS SUPPOSED TO MEET US TODAY.

LET'S GIVE IT A GO.

Enter a date in mm-dd format: 06-03

Enter a date in mm-dd format: 06-03

JUNIOR MUSIC ROOM

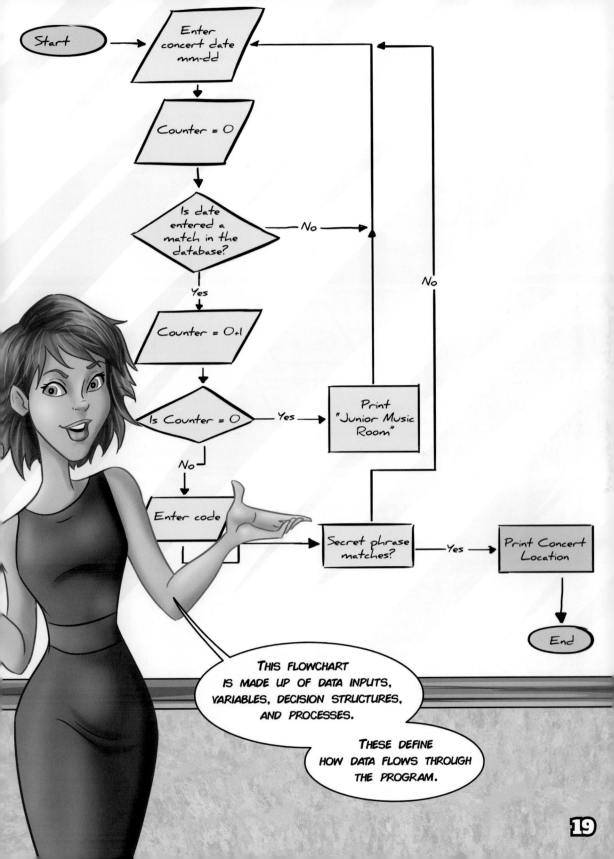

Start

Enter concert date mm-dd

Counter = 0

Is date entered a match in the database? — No

Yes

Counter = 0+1

Is Counter = 0 — Yes → Print "Junior Music Room"

No

Enter code

Secret phrase matches? — Yes → Print Concert Location

End

No

THIS FLOWCHART IS MADE UP OF DATA INPUTS, VARIABLES, DECISION STRUCTURES, AND PROCESSES.

THESE DEFINE HOW DATA FLOWS THROUGH THE PROGRAM.

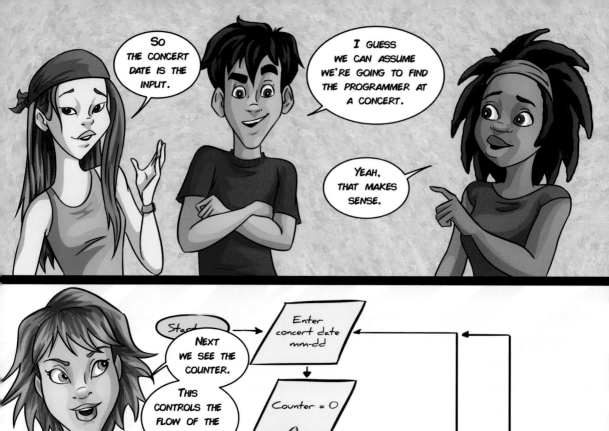

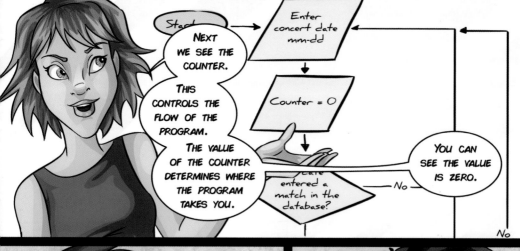

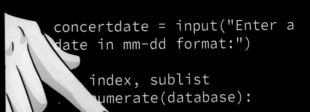

```
concertdate = input("Enter a
date in mm-dd format:")

    index, sublist
    enumerate(database):

    if sublist[0] == concertdate:

    if (counter ==0):

    print("Junior Music Room")
```

```
for index, sublist
in enumerate(database):

counter +=1

if sublist[0] == concertdate:
```

```
Enter a date in mm-dd format: 06-03

ENTER CODE:
```

```
Enter a date in mm-dd format: 06-03

ENTER CODE: PYTHON
```

```
ENTER CODE: PYTHON

No match, try again.
```

Enter a date in mm-dd format: 06-03

ENTER CODE: 16252081514

Enter a date in mm-dd format: 06-03

ENTER CODE: 16252081514

Grant Park Bandstand

FREE CONCERT
June 3rd
5pm
Grant Park

4:30PM

LOOKS LIKE WE'LL BE GOING TO THAT CONCERT AFTER ALL.

ALL WE HAVE TO DO IS SHOW UP AND WE'LL FIND THE MISSING PROGRAMMER!

I'LL FINALLY GET MY AUTOGRAPH FROM SAM NORTH!

COOL! I HOPE THEY LET DOGS IN.

WOOF!

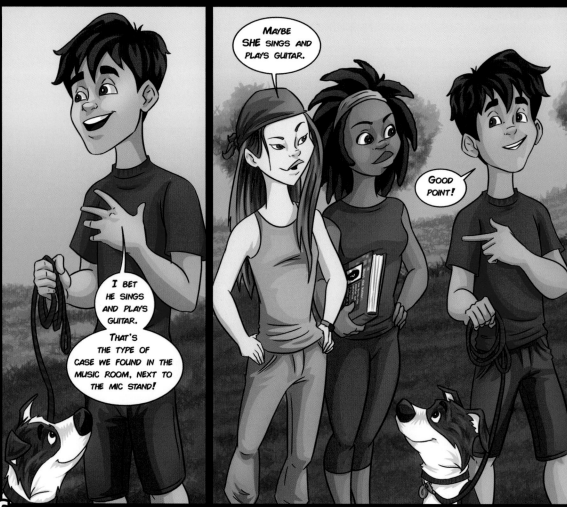

This first song is called "Crack the Code."

I dedicate it to you, Power Coders!

Sam North! We found you!

I CAN'T BE EVERYWHERE, SO I LEFT YOU MY CALLING CARD.

THANK YOU! THIS IS SO COOL.

Bug Fixing

Sam North

AMAZING WORK SOLVING MY MYSTERY. IT WASN'T SO EASY.

BUT IT WAS WORTH IT! THAT WAS A GREAT CONCERT!

WOOF!